Pra

M000295904

"*Mandy Haynes effortlessly and brilliantly writes children, a feat at which many writers struggle and fail. In Oliver, her uniquely, lyrical voice sings the reader smack dab into this heartwarming story inhabited by Oliver and Olivia, a brother and sister whose special bond is symbiotically balanced upon the other's abilities and perspectives. I dare you to not fall immediately in love with these characters, and fret over them as I did as they make their journey through this poignant summer from long ago.*"

Robert Gwaltney, author of *The Cicada Tree*

"*A small-town story of childhood innocence, sibling admiration, blind optimism, and plenty of shenanigans, author Mandy Haynes has penned an incomparable narrator in Sissy, who tells a multifaceted story highlighting the altruistic plans of her remarkable brother, Oliver. The Southern jargon in this charming novella is character defining, the precocious mood insightful. Oliver is about bringing out the goodness in people, even if it takes a bit of magic.*"

Claire Fullerton, author of *Little Tea*

"Mandy Haynes takes me on a memory journey to the last great childhood of the South, a time when bicycles were a magic carpet that could take a child wherever she wanted to go. The joy of this novella is how easily I slip between the pages and live the adventures with Oliver and Olivia. Sibling love. Kindness. Good intentions gone awry and good deeds fraught with danger. This story echos with my past, and the past of many now homeless Southerners. Once you start reading, you won't be able to put it down."

Carolyn Haines, USA Today bestseller, is the author of over 80 books in multiple genres

Additional Praise for Mandy Haynes

"Mandy Haynes gives us a direct line into the heart of the Deep South. To understand what is genteel and genuine, one must also understand what is not. Strong female characters who get the better of villains who seek to destroy them abound in this brilliantly crafted collection of short stories. She is Flannery O'Connor's equal in the new millennium."
Marci Henna, author of *When We Last Spoke*

"Mandy Haynes captures the authentic southern stories readers love. She writes, not with stereotypes readers can spot from a mile away, but with wisdom which comes from the calloused hands of a great author."
Renea Winchester, author of *Outbound Train*

"For fans who loved the young narrator, Peejoe, along with Aunt Lucille, in Mark Childress's bestselling novel, Crazy In Alabama, you will love the hardscrabble and inquisitive narrators in Mandy Haynes's collection."
Kathleen M. Rodgers, author of *The Flying Cutterbucks*

"What a cast of characters! What a voice! And what insight and empathy into the lives of her diverse characters. I am a huge Mandy Haynes fan. I see in her writing traces of Flannery O'Conner and Alice Munro. Having read both of her short story collections, Walking the Wrong Way Home and Sharp as a Serpent's Tooth, I find myself thinking of her characters long after closing the book."
Debra Thomas, author of *Luz*

"Mandy Haynes never shies away from the hard truths of rough living. She's casting into the weeds, where silt-dwellers are circled by dragonflies, their brilliant sapphire blues and the lace of their wings darting and emerging, like Haynes' tales, from all six directions, and with redemptive grace."
Suzanne Hudson, prize winning author of 2018's *Shoe-Burnin' Season: A Womanifesto* (pseudonym R.P. Saffire) and 2019's *The Fall of the Nixon Administration*, a comic novel

"It may be fiction but it's all true. Mandy writes razor-sharp, down-to-the bone southern tales about total strangers that you've known your whole life. She knows us better than we know ourselves. This is the good stuff." Mike Henderson, Grammy award winning singer/ songwriter, musician, and all around badass

"Reading Mandy Haynes's collection of short stories, Sharp as a Serpent's Tooth, takes me on a journey down red clay backroads to the gothic South where Flannery O'Connor rides shotgun and whispers in my ear. Haynes takes her fiction into a world I love--a South of conmen, snake handlers, and individuals with unsettling courage. She brings fresh insight into characters I've met and places I've visited in real life and in fiction. There's no better journey-- highly recommended."

USA Today bestselling author Carolyn Haines, 2010 Harper Lee Distinguished Writer Award winner

"Mandy Haynes has written the most beautiful collection of stories I have read in a very long time. She has a unique talent for awakening empathy and compassion in the reader with her language, nuance, and detail. Each of her characters is so completely human and real that the reader is caught up in their eperiences, their challenges, and their lessons while also discovering lessons and insights about themselves and their own personal humanity. I found my heart breaking, my gut wrenching, my tears falling, and my mouth cheering them on as I was immersed in each story."

Kathryn Taylor, author of *Two Minus One*: A Memoir

"I was drawn in from the first sentence of the first story and it didn't let me go until the last sentence of the final story. I even read the acknowledgments to keep from having to close the book for a final time. The stories are set in the South but the plights are universal, the characters are people you pass on the road each day but fail to notice, and the stakes are simple, yet life-encompassing. The voices of these characters and the twists and turns of these stories will stay with you for a very long time."

Amazon Reader review

"This collection of short stories should be on the bookshelf of every women's shelter, every therapy center, every home. How Ms Haynes managed to come from a place of humorous yet deep empowerment as she shares the freedom journeys of her characters without downplaying their need to find their homes is both insightful and inspiring.

The stories are told in the easy Southern rhythm that catches hold of your heart before you're through the first paragraph. Each story is a stand-alone book in its own right, so like a buffet, you can skip around to fill your plate with what catches your eye... but you will be back to refill that plate again and again.

Best read with a water-beaded glass of lemonade or sweet tea with your feet up and your heart open. Excellent book for gift giving."

Amazon Reader Review

"I am not a book critic. I am a voracious reader, but I read strictly for pleasure and escape. I've hesitated to write a review, but as crazy 2020 evolves into even crazier 2021, I have to say that both of Mandy's books have been a tremendous comfort and escape for me. I love her gentle Southern voice, and her strong Southern female style. I highly, highly recommend these books of short stories. They have been delightful and perfect."

Amazon Reader Review

"These are more than stories, these are tales of what it's like to be human, to live in this world with all its loves and sadness, beauty and ugliness. She's turned what should be her own unique stories and made them universal, something that sounds new and yet hauntingly familiar."

Kathleen Cosgrove, author of Engulfed

"Wonderful stories. Brilliantly written. Some hopeful. Some sad. All riveting. Intelligent, and yet really creative style. Among the best of short story authors out there. Powerful insights into the complexities of human and family relationships."
Amazon Reader Review

"I love Mandy Haynes' work. The stories in "Walking the Wrong Way Home" are exquisitely written, and I had to slow myself down as I didn't want to finish the collection. The characters stayed with me, and I was reminded of Louise Erdich's work, where the characters feel actual, and I care about them. I can't wait to read more."
Amazon Reader Review

"In these pages I "saw" people I knew from my past, though I don't know the author nor the characters. In these pages I recognized my own dreams and memories. Mandy has mined the human experience perfectly! Definitely recommend."
Amazon Reader Review

OLIVER

a novella

Mandy Haynes

Also by Mandy Haynes

Walking the Wrong Way Home

*Sharp as a Serpent's Tooth -Eva and
Other Stories*

Work In Progress

Copyright © 2022 by Mandy Haynes

Oliver is a work of fiction. Any resemblance to persons living or dead is coincidental.

No crawdads or puppies were injured in the writing of these stories.

Published by three dogs write press

First Edition 2022

ISBN 978-1-7334675-5-1

Cover Design by Mandy Haynes
@ three dogs write press

Dedicated to my grandsons,
Cannon and Holden Groves.
I hope you always see the magic.

Table of Contents

Chapter One

"He's the nice one – I'm the onery one in the family..."

The biggest mistake most people make is thinking that my brother, Oliver, is stupid. He ain't. He's one of the smartest boys I ever met. I know dern good and well he can read better than Eli Jones and Eli made it to the eleventh grade. It ain't Oliver's fault they wouldn't let him go past Junior High. It was the school's fault for not stopping the boys that bullied him. But since those boys were also the best Defensive Tackles on the football team, they got away with everything. Especially Delbert and Gilbert Jones. Their daddy's picture was in a case beside some big stupid trophy in the lobby of the High School, so they thought they ruled the whole school. Shoot, they thought they ruled the whole town.

The way everybody worshipped football should've been a sin but that would mean Preacher Mark was a sinner too. Every Friday night during football season you'd find him in the stands, wearing his old jersey, hollering and shouting for the Wildcats to beat the snot out of the opposing team. On Sunday before a big game he had a special prayer just for the team—and not for their souls neither – just for the win. It always got on my last nerve. But then a lot of things got on my nerves – like the tiny dumb pans that came with my Easy Bake Oven and how the kids in my class acted like they were too old for The Electric Company when I knew for a fact they still watched it.

The day the school called the meeting with Mama and Daddy to tell them they thought Oliver had "advanced" as far as he would and said he shouldn't come back the following year, I know it was because Oliver finally stood his ground against the twins. He'd punched Gilbert in the stomach and Delbert in the nose and left them both lying on the sidewalk. One punch was all it took to turn the two biggest players on the team into crying babies. One punch. If the coaches at East Robertson or Portland High School heard about it, they'd use it against the Wildcats. They couldn't have that, so of course the boys made up stories about Oliver.

Gilbert and Delbert's daddy went to the school board and said Oliver was a danger to the other students and a liability to the school, like he was some kind of crazy person or had special evil powers or something. Everybody knew it was a load of horse crap, because Oliver didn't have a mean bone in his body. He's the nice one – I'm the onery one in the family with the short temper and I don't mind a fight. Sometimes I guess you could say I even like them...Not Oliver. He'd given those dumbos plenty of chances the whole year to leave him alone. But when they pushed him into the girl's bathroom it embarrassed Laura Lee so bad she'd locked herself in a stall and bawled her eyes out. He didn't attack them because he was an out of control lunatic, he'd been taking up for Laura Lee. And he didn't have some freaky super human strength neither, those boys were just wimps.

Anyway, when the coaches at our school couldn't talk Oliver into playing football they didn't care what happened to him. And just for the record, nobody cared anything about Laura Lee neither. Nobody except Oliver.

Oliver cared about everybody. But he didn't care about a diploma. He didn't need one to work on our farm with Daddy, so quitting school wasn't a big deal for him. It wasn't like he had a lot of friends there anyway.

Shoot, I wanted to quit too, but I was a girl and three years younger than my brother. My aunts told me if I didn't finish school I'd have to get married when I turned twenty. Since both of them were married and neither of them seemed to like it too much, I figured school was the way to go. I didn't need some bossy man telling me when to wash his clothes or what to cook for supper. No, thank you. Even if twenty seemed a long ways off I knew I wouldn't change my mind – not in eight years and probably never. So I go to school and don't raise too much of a fuss about it. Not that I don't play hooky when the crappie are biting, but I don't miss enough days to give my mama a reason to notice.

But it did make me mad that they didn't think Oliver was smart enough to get a diploma even if it didn't bother Oliver none. He liked helping Daddy raise tobacco and hay on our farm and he had a big garden he took care of all by himself. I didn't like weeding, but I'd help him pick when it was time to and help him sell tomatoes and squash and whatever else he grew over the summer. He paid me good, so I had my own money to buy root beer floats, comics, and movie tickets, which made it worth the hot hours I put in. Plus I liked delivering tomatoes and squash to the ladies who lived in the little row of houses across the railroad tracks. They were a hoot and always had sweet tea for us when we stopped by so sometimes we didn't charge them anything if we had extra or the tomatoes were starting to get soft.

Oliver made money – he even had his own savings account at the bank, so I guess it didn't really matter. But it still irked me that those two dufuses were probably going to go to college in Knoxville on a football scholarship when they were both dumber than rocks.

My brother was a small for his age, but he was solid muscle, and his hands were as calloused as men twice his age, even though he was just a kid and would always be. Or so those doctors said. They had a name for what was wrong with Oliver, but Mama and Daddy never used it. I spent a lot of time looking at kids in my class trying to figure out what was wrong with them because it was clear as spring water, half of them weren't near as smart as Oliver.

Sometimes I looked at myself in the mirror and wondered the same thing. Maybe we were the ones that had something wrong with us, and people like Oliver who looked or acted a little bit different were the "normal" ones.

If y'all think I'm exaggerating about how smart Oliver is, I'm going to share a story and you can see what I'm talking about. Something happened last summer that proves Oliver is special. And I don't mean "special" like other people mean when they look at Oliver. I mean special like there ain't nobody like him.

Chapter Two

"Sissy, you ready?"

We were down at the drugstore for our ice cream float fix, when Oliver pointed out to me how Ms. Linda would bat her eyelashes and get all pink in the face when Mr. Trey came in.

"I think she's sweet on him." Oliver chuckled before turning his attention to the last of the root beer in his glass.

I'd never noticed, but once Oliver pointed it out, I couldn't not see it. He was right. Ms. Linda looked like Bugs Bunny when he put on those long eyelashes. Her eyes were extra shiny and her cheeks almost glowed. I half expected to see little fake hearts and bluebirds pop up out of nowhere and start circling Mr. Trey's head.

"And I think he's kinda sweet on her." Oliver turned all the way around to get a better look. "Every time we're here he's here."

"Well are you sweet on her too? 'Cause every time he's here so are you."

I nudged him in the shin with the toe of my shoe to get him to turn back around.

"Sissy, we can't get root beer floats anywhere but here." He rolled his eyes at me. "Mr. Trey walks past two other places where he could get coffee to come to Ms. Linda's Diner." Oliver grinned, "And they have coffee in the lobby, right outside his office."

Oliver was right. Mr. Trey worked at the bank three blocks away and they did have coffee…Mama always had a cup when there was a line in front of her favorite teller instead of going to someone else. She only liked going to Nancy's window because she played bridge with Nancy's mama and Nancy always told whoever was there what a great bridge player Mama was. She'd always act embarrassed but man, she loved it.

"Dang, do you think he comes here every day?" Oliver nodded and chased the last bit of root beer around the bottom of the glass with his straw.

I had to hurry to catch up with him which caused one of those horrible brain freeze pains to shoot up my forehead to the ends of my hair. I still had ice cream in my float because I'd been too busy staring at Ms. Linda to eat it. If I didn't hurry, Oliver would be ready to go, and I'd have to leave before I finished the best part. I ignored the pain and used a spoon to scoop up the fluffy half-melted ice cream chunks when Oliver's straw started making loud air-sucking-up noises.

"Sissy, you ready?" Oliver asked, standing up before I could answer. I dropped the spoon and turned the glass up, determined to get every last ice cream cloud drop even if it meant having a spasm.

"Bye, Ms. Linda!" Oliver hollered as he pushed the door open, and I flinched.

"Dang, inside voice Oliver," I reminded him for the thousandth time. His goodbyes were always loud – like he was going away for a year or something –and I'd been caught in the middle because I wasn't paying attention. Instead of ducking, I was concentrating on pressing my thumb to the roof of my mouth to stop my brain from freezing.

"See you two on Thursday," she said and smiled at us before she went back to blushing over Mr. Trey.

"I think they're boyfriend and girlfriend," Oliver informed me as we saddled our bikes and headed towards the library.

"Duh," I answered, even though it had never once crossed my mind until five minutes ago.

"They're probably smooching right now." I made kissy noises on the back of my hand until I about ran into a light pole.

We laughed ourselves silly all the way to the library, but once we opened the doors that led to shelves and shelves of beautiful books we got serious.

I kept a list of books I wanted, and I'd been waiting for weeks for A Wrinkle in Time to be returned. If it wasn't there The Island of the Blue Dolphins was next on the list and if that wasn't available, I'd just reread any Nancy Drew, or Hardy Boys book until they came back, but if Charlene Brown didn't hurry up and return A Wrinkle in Time I was going to go to her house and get it myself. I took my list seriously. But not Oliver, he never knew what he was going to take home until we left. Mrs. Catherine Clark, the librarian and one of the best storytellers in the whole world, would have something picked out and waiting for him at the desk. No matter what it was he never asked for anything different because he said she always knew the perfect one.

The books she picked out for Oliver weren't ones I'd ever pick for myself. They looked boring, like schoolbooks, but they weren't – some of them were even more interesting than Nancy Drew but I'd never admit it. Whenever Oliver asked me to read something interesting from one of them I always acted like it was a chore, even though secretly I liked it. But I didn't have to read them because Oliver soaked every story up like a sponge.

Trust me, if you were to ask him about the Cherokee Indians who once lived over in East Tennessee, the Wright Brothers, or about the old Presidents of the United States he'd tell you more than you ever wanted to know and teach you a few things you never learned in school.

Did you know that John Quincy Adams used to go skinny dipping in the Potomac River?

Me neither.

Chapter Three

"More coffee?"

The following Thursday I helped Oliver finish his list of things to do so we could get to Linda's Diner early. I wanted to beat Mr. Trey and see what it was like when he walked in the door. Because that dang Charlene was still hogging A Wrinkle in Time and somebody else beat me to my second choice, I'd picked the newest Nancy Drew book, The Secret of Mirror Bay. I'd already read it three times over, and I couldn't concentrate. All I could think about was what Oliver pointed out. I was convinced Mr. Trey and Ms. Linda were already all talked out by the time we usually got there, or they passed notes or something. Instead of sitting at our usual table by the windows where we watched everybody on Main Street, we took a stool at the counter so we could be closer to the real action.

When Mr. Trey walked in and smiled at Ms. Linda, Oliver and I burst out laughing.

"Oliver that's the funniest joke I've ever heard!" I slapped the counter and put the other hand on my chest.

"I didn't..." My brother quit laughing and wrinkled his eyebrows together until they almost touched.

I pretended my foot slipped off the rail of my stool and kicked him in the ankle. Oliver's eyebrows shot up in surprise, then even higher as he understood what was going on. He answered with a fake belly laugh that got me so tickled I slapped the counter again, but as soon as Mr. Trey took off his hat we got quiet so we wouldn't miss anything.

But there wasn't anything to miss. Ms. Linda got him a cup of coffee and a piece of pie without even saying anything. Not even hello. When she finally said something it was nothing more than, "More coffee?" which got a nod from Mr. Trey, and "It looks like we're going to get some rain on Monday." Blah, blah, blah. I looked for any secret signals they might be giving each other but they hardly even made eye contact.

It was so boring I quickly lost interest. Maybe we'd been wrong – maybe Mr. Trey really did like the coffee here. I whispered to Oliver that I wanted to scoot down to a stool by the window to find something more exciting to focus on – like bird poop on the statue of the old guy who fought in the civil war, or paint peeling off the window trim – but Oliver wasn't ready to leave. He swatted me away and studied them like he was going to write a paper on how to act like boring adults or something.

Mr. Trey was a nice man and didn't take offense at Oliver staring. Instead, he smiled at my brother and asked, "How's your daddy doing?"

"He's good."

"Y'all put out some nice tobacco, how's it doing?"

"It's good," Oliver grinned. "It'll be ready to cut soon."

"And then the hard work starts, I reckon." Mr. Trey shook his head. "I've hung tobacco myself when I was younger. Most people have no idea how much work goes into it, do they?"

Oliver kept grinning, "No, sir, they don't."

"How's Loretta?"

Oliver beamed at the mention of her name.

Loretta was my brother's beagle and the best rabbit dog in Middle Tennessee. She stayed out on our Uncle Woodard's farm where he turned a whole horse barn into a kennel just for her and her pups. I slid off the stool and went to the window because I knew we'd be here a while. Oliver loved talking about Loretta more than he did tobacco plants or Andrew Jackson's run-in with the Bell Witch.

They talked about everything from Loretta's last litter to the eight-point buck Oliver shot two years ago while I watched Ms. Linda's reflection in the glass watching Mr. Trey.

I turned from the window and tried to send telepathic messages to them, but all it did was make my head hurt. Mr. Trey didn't seem to have any trouble talking to my brother—so why couldn't he talk to Ms. Linda?

"Oh, look at the time. I've got to get back work," Mr. Trey said to Oliver. My brother surprised us all by pointing out to Mr. Trey how pretty Ms. Linda's lips were.

"She has a nice smile, don't she, Mr. Trey? Her lips are always so shiny and they're a nice shade of pink. Like, almost natural, but fancier."

Oliver

My brother smiled at Ms. Linda and looked back at Mr. Trey.

"Don't you think?"

"Well, yes, she—why, I don't, I mean, I guess…"

Poor guy. He'd turned so red I thought he was going to burst into flames. He had trouble getting his money out of his pocket and ended up pulling the whole thing inside out. Coins went bouncing all over the place and when he jumped off his stool to bend down to get them, he almost whacked his head on the counter.

I felt plumb sorry for him, so I helped him round up the pennies that rolled my way and tried not to grin. When he picked up all the change, he put the whole handful on the counter and left without saying anything. He was in such a hurry to get away that he left his hat on the stool beside Oliver.

As soon as the door closed behind Mr. Trey, Ms. Linda leaned over the counter and ruffled Oliver's hair. When she smiled, I saw that Oliver was right. She did have pretty lips. I'd never noticed.

Oliver grinned and we put our money on the counter to pay for our floats, but she slid it back towards us.

"This round's on me, kiddos." She winked and it was Oliver's turn to blush.

"Thanks, Ms. Linda," I said putting my money back in my pocket, but Oliver left his dollar on the counter.

When he stood up, he slid Mr. Trey's hat off the stool and knelt down like he was tying his shoe. But it was already tied… Before he stood up he snuck the hat behind his back.

What are you—" I started to ask but he cut me off.

"Come on, Sissy, we've got to go." He started walking backwards and I realized he was waiting on me to open the door.

Chapter Four

"If anybody asks, we'll tell the truth."

"What are you doing?" I whispered once we got outside. I looked over my shoulder even though nobody was around.

"I don't know, but I bet we can think of something." He put the hat in the basket attached to the handlebars on my bike, careful not to bend the brim. I wanted to pick it up and put it on, but I was too chicken. Nobody, except Mr. Trey, wore hats like that if they weren't in the movies.

"Hey, Oliver, why do you think Mr. Trey wears this old thing anyway? I mean he looks pretty good in it, but it's kind of weird, ain't it?

Oliver shrugged. "Maybe it was his Daddy's or something – or maybe he's just old fashioned."

"That would explain why he's so proper around Ms. Linda." I laughed, but Oliver didn't see anything funny.

We pedaled for a few minutes without saying anything and I listened to the clicking sound of the Ace of Spades against the spokes of my wheel, waiting for Oliver to tell me what he was up to. I liked the nickname Ace, but Oliver refused to call me anything but Sissy. He says it's not a nickname because it's who I am, his Sissy. Mama said he's called me that since the day I came home from the hospital. I didn't mind, except when he said it in front of Eli Jones because he always repeated it like you sissy, and thought it was hilarious.

"Wonder why Mr. Trey didn't tell Ms. Linda he thought she was pretty?" Oliver asked. "Everybody thinks she's pretty. It's not a secret."

I shook my head, "Why didn't Ms. Linda ask him anything except if he wanted more coffee? Did you notice she didn't even ask if he wanted pie? She just gives him the same thing every time without asking if that's what he wants." I tried to picture the first time he ordered something from her. Did he write his order on a napkin or did he get up the courage to say it out loud?

"Sometimes she gives him apple pie..." Oliver said it like it made a difference. "And once she gave him a piece of chocolate cake."

"She should ask Mr. Trey to the movies. I know she likes to go because we see her just about every time we go to the matinee."

Oliver agreed. I wasn't exaggerating; Ms. Linda was always at the matinee, always alone, but always dressed up like she wasn't. Like she was meeting somebody for a date, but I never saw anybody buy her ticket or share her popcorn. She always sat in the fourth row up from the bottom, dead center. I knew because Mama liked to sit in the fifth row up from the bottom, six seats in from the left.

"I got an idea!" Oliver shouted and then he told me all about it the rest of the way home.

We had the whole thing figured out by the time we pulled into the driveway. It was a great plan, and I was feeling pretty proud of us for coming up with it. We were going to leave Mr. Trey's hat on his porch with Ms. Linda's phone number stuck in the band. He'd think she was the one who left it and he'd have to call her to thank her. Just in case he couldn't think of anything to say, we were going to leave some flowers on the doorstep at the Diner with a note from Mr. Trey thanking Linda for returning the hat. We figured that when Mr. Trey got up the nerve to call her, she'd thank him for the flowers, he'd thank her for his hat, and they'd both forget that neither one of them did those things - or be too embarrassed to admit it, anyway.

But my excitement started to turn in to anxiety as soon as we reached the back porch.

"What if it doesn't work?"

"Mr. Trey will have his hat back." Oliver grinned, "The rest is up to them."

"But do you think we might get in trouble?" I asked. "I mean, we're kind of lying, ain't we?"

Oliver looked at the hat for a minute, thinking hard. "Naw, we're just telling a story. That's different than lying."

I didn't answer, I was thinking of the last time Mama had threatened me with a switch for telling stories. Oliver must've read my mind.

"This ain't a story to keep from getting in trouble. If anybody asks, we'll tell the truth." He laughed at the look on my face. "Olivia, this is different than telling Mama you tripped and accidentally hit Eli in the nose when you charged him like a bull on the steps of the school."

He poked me with his elbow. "In front of everybody, including Principal Witherspoon."

"What was I supposed to do?" I clenched my fists. Just thinking about Eli Jones made me mad enough to spit nails. "Anyway, I was aiming for his big fat mouth, so hitting him in the nose was an accident. His stupid foot tripped me right before I could knock his big ugly teeth out."

Oliver thought it was funny when I got mad, which was a lot of the time. In my defense, I had twice as much of a temper because Oliver didn't have any. It wasn't my fault I'd ended up with his and mine. After he stopped laughing he said, "If it doesn't work, we'll tell the truth. We got bored watching them not talk to each other and we were just trying to help."

I rolled my eyes and sighed. "If it don't work you do the talking."

I made him pinky swear that I wouldn't have to do the explaining before we walked around to the back of the house.

"Let's get busy before Mama comes looking for us," Oliver said. He got the pair of kitchen shears mama used to cut the flowers she grew in flower beds all around the house and trees. Daddy teased her that they weren't going to have any grass left to call a yard if she didn't watch out. She kept the shears hanging from a little hook like ones people used to hang coffee cups under a cupboard. Everything around her potting table was organized, just like her kitchen. She had a whole row of hooks holding all kinds of things. A roll of twine, a twist of copper wire, a strand of dried peppers she never did nothing with, but they looked pretty, and paper envelopes with holes punched in the flaps. One of the envelopes hung open, stuffed full of marigold and zinnia seeds from when she deadheaded her flowers. Next spring she'd plant what she had in the envelope and do the same thing all over again.

We walked to Mama's side garden and got busy gathering roses for Ms. Linda.

I help up the fistful of pink and red roses and shook my head.

"What's wrong?" Oliver asked.

"We don't have a vase. How are we supposed to make a fancy flower arrangement without a vase?"

Oliver ran to the back porch and got one of mama's canning jars she'd set out to dry on a towel. He stopped to fill it with water from the hosepipe before handing it to me.

"What about this?" He smiled, and I

couldn't help but smile back. When Oliver smiled his whole face smiled at you.

"Perfect." I said and meant it. I thought they looked real pretty in the quart-sized jar. I walked over to the side yard and snipped some Queen Anne's Lace from the edge of our property. Even though people called it chigger weed and swore it was full biting bugs, it was my favorite flower. The blooms reminded me of the crocheted lace dollies my aunts made. I added some fern spikes and a couple of wild daisies to fill in the bare spots and asked Oliver what he thought.

"Good job, Sissy," he said. He took the jar and hid it with Mr. Trey's hat under the Holly bush at the corner of the house.

"Let's get some lemonade. All this planning made me thirsty," I said, feeling pretty big in the britches until I walked in the kitchen and ran smack dab into Mama.

"Olivia, what kind of mischief are you up to now?" Mama raised an eyebrow, and I almost spilled my guts. Sometimes I swear she could see right into my mind.

But Oliver was quick. He opened the refrigerator and started rooting around. It worked – Mama couldn't stand anybody poking around in the kitchen when she was cooking supper. She forgot about me and shooed us out without asking more questions and Oliver and I went on to the next part of our plan, forgetting we were thirsty.

Chapter Five

We were two real life Cupids minus the diapers and bow and arrows.

"There it is," I almost shouted, "643-2076."

Ms. Linda's number was easy to find; she was the only Espeleta listed in the phone book. I wrote her number on a piece of pink paper from Mama's stationery, careful to make sure my three didn't look like an eight and that my seven didn't look like a one. Then I wrote "You left your hat at the diner" taking my time to write real fancy.

"Should I make the dot on top of the i a heart?" I asked but decided not to before Oliver answered. If the truth came out that I'd written the letter I didn't want Mr. Trey to get the wrong idea and think I was a girly-girl or worse, that I secretly had a crush on him.

Oliver wanted to spray some of Mama's perfume on the letter, but I wouldn't let him. I thought that was pushing it a little too far. Besides, Mama would know we were up to something if we sat down to dinner smelling like White Shoulders perfume.

Then I took a plain piece of white paper and wrote a quick thank you on it, hoping that it would pass for a grown man's handwriting. After five attempts I was getting aggravated, but Oliver took the pencil from me and got it perfect on the first try.

I went back in the kitchen to make sure Mama wasn't looking out the window while Oliver took the thank you note and number out to the Holly bush to hide with the hat and the flowers. He tiptoed back in the front door without getting caught but I wasn't so lucky.

"Olivia! You startled me." Mama jumped when she turned and saw me standing at the sink. She'd been so busy fussing with her pot roast she hadn't heard me come in. "What are you doing just standing there?"

"Nothin'. Just came down to see what was for supper."

Oliver

"Really? It's roast. Same as every Wednesday." She tried the eyebrow trick again, but this time I didn't even wince, not even when she flared her nostrils. Three seconds went by before she made them their normal size again and I kept myself calm by imaging sticking a quarter in her right nostril to see if it fits. I don't know why she always gave me a hard time, I'd never seen her flare those things at Oliver once.

"Since you're here you can give me a hand setting the table. Get the blue napkins, please - and tell Oliver to get washed up. Your daddy should be home in five minutes, and I want to sit down in ten."

"Yes, ma'am," I hurried to get the blue cloth napkins from the new cabinet Mama called a sideboard in the dining room, thankful to get out of the kitchen and out from under the pressure of her eyebrow. I imagined that's what the bad guys felt like when they were forced to sit under the glare of a naked light bulb while being interrogated.

Sitting at the table was more nerve wrecking than I expected. I suffered from a guilty conscience, but Oliver wasn't the best at keeping secrets. He couldn't help himself - Mama had learned to keep my birthday and my Christmas presents a surprise for both me and Oliver. If it was something fun he had to share, and our secret was a fun one. We were two real life Cupids minus the diapers and bow and arrows. I'd been so worried about me telling on myself I hadn't thought about Oliver.

Somehow we got through supper without spilling the beans—well, except for the ones on Oliver's plate. He always made a mess. To be honest, I wasn't that neat either. I was just better at hiding crumbs and things under the edge of my plate. There was also a little space, a ledge under the table around the top, where I used to hide things like brussel sprouts and butter beans until Mama found it last spring when she decided to give the entire table a lemon oil treatment. Trust me, that had not been a good day.

"Mama, me and Oliver will clean up the kitchen," I blurted out, "you and Daddy go on in the living room."

"Well, Olivia, that's awful nice of you," Mama looked so surprised it almost hurt my feelings. "I think I'll take you up on that."

We were lucky her favorite show was about to come on. If it'd been any other night, she would've insisted on washing the dishes and we'd be stuck in the kitchen together. I'd been able to avoid eye contact at the table but there was no way I'd be able to do that if we were washing and drying dishes together. I held my breath as Mama patted Oliver's shoulder and smiled at Daddy who held his arm out to her.

"Thanks, kids," Daddy said, and I nodded with that goofy smile plastered across my face until they were in the next room.

Once Oliver and I were alone I let out a breath so big it blew his bangs off his forehead. We rushed to clean the dining room table off so we could get in the kitchen and put another wall between us for privacy. Then we talked about the rest of our plan as we stood side by side at the sink and washed every dish until they shined.

This was a good idea, Sissy," Oliver said as he put the last clean plate in the cabinet.

"Yeah. I figure if we do get caught Mama might remember how good we've been."

"No, I mean we should do this more. Let Mama sit down after supper and do this ourselves."

"Oh," I looked around the kitchen and thought of all over the other places I'd rather be than there.

"Sure," I said, "maybe special occasions like Mother's Day or her birthday."

"Come on, Sissy. It wouldn't kill you."

I jabbed him in the ribs and giggled, "Hey, like Ms. Penny says - we cain't all be saints."

Chapter Six

The Night Stalker but without the vampires.

We'd decided to wait until half past ten to leave the house, but I was worried it wouldn't be late enough since Mama and Daddy never went to bed until the weather report.

"Thirty minutes is plenty of time for them to fall asleep," Oliver said, and I'll be danged if he wasn't right. We heard Daddy's snores coming from their room at the end of the hall at exactly ten thirty.

Oliver and I had both gotten under our covers fully dressed so we'd be ready to go. We slipped on our shoes, tiptoed down the hall, through the kitchen, and out the back door. I was too scared to breathe until we reached the bottom step and I wasn't sure if I felt dizzy from the lack of oxygen or excitement. I'd never snuck out of the house at night before. I took a couple of deep breaths to calm myself, but I almost messed everything up when I stuck my arm under the Holly bush and it went in a spider's web. I bit my lip to keep from squealing and fell back on my butt, slapping my arms and rolling around like a pig in a puddle. Oliver clamped his hand over his mouth to keep from laughing out loud and put his other hand on my foot. He gave it a yank and I came to my senses, sure I'd woken everybody on our street. We stayed hunched down waiting for Daddy to come out and catch us.

"Listen," Oliver whispered after he stopped laughing. I heard Daddy's rumbling snore through the kitchen window.

"How does Mama sleep with all that noise coming out of him? He sounds like a freight train barreling through a tunnel," I whispered. Oliver reached through the remnants of the spider's web for the hat and flowers without flinching. A shiver shot down my back at the thought. I would rather stick my hand in a nest of snakes than have one spider crawl on me.

Once we had everything placed in the basket we sped off on our bikes and put our plan into action.

We stopped at Mr. Trey's house first since it was on the way. Everything was going just like we planned, but we almost blew it when a grey cat jumped out from his hiding place behind a porch post. Oliver yelped in surprise, threw the hat, and crouched down behind the porch railings. The hat landed right on top of the stray, and he took off with the fedora. I thought we were goners, but it fell off right in front of the door before the cat jumped in the bushes.

Oliver waited a couple of seconds before he stood up and gave me a wave. Then he tiptoed up to the porch and checked to make sure the note was still there. He gave me a thumbs up before he ran to the curb where I was waiting with the bikes.

"Who knew we'd have to fight off killer spiders and panthers. What's next?" I asked.

Oliver giggled and I knew what was coming. "Vam…"

"Stop it, Oliver! That's not funny." I pedaled faster to get in front of him but changed my mind when I saw the shadows from the big oak trees reaching across the street. I touched the brakes and let him get beside me. I'd had nightmares for a month after sneaking out of bed to watch The Night Stalker. Everybody at school had talked about how they couldn't wait for the ABC Movie of the Week. I was excited too, but when it came on, Mama said I was too young and my imagination was too wild to watch it and sent me to bed. I had to sneak to my hiding place behind the sofa to see the TV. I should've listened to her.

"Sissy, I'll stop teasing." Oliver swerved his front tire into mine and it felt like our bikes were giving each other high fives.

I forgave him and we rode side by side the rest of the way to the diner.

Everything looked so different at nighttime. Nobody was driving down the street, so we rode right in the middle. I looked at all the dark windows in the houses we passed and wondered what everyone inside was dreaming about. When we got to town, I looked at the store windows and wondered if the cat that lived inside A.J.'s Hardware Store was doing his job and keeping the mice out of the birdseed or if they were playing hide and seek instead. Maybe they were friends who had a deal - like the mice only ate the loose seed and stayed out of the bags. And the cat shared the water in his dish when they were thirsty.

We stopped in front of Linda's Diner and Oliver placed the flowers on the step without any spider, cat, or vampire attacks and we made our way back home feeling pretty good about what we'd accomplished.

"This is fun Oliv…"

A pair of headlights came out of nowhere and whatever they were attached to was flying towards us, charging down the wrong side of the road. Oliver and I got out of the way right before we were smashed flat.

"Watch out ahole!" I yelled and flipped the driver a bird as he passed, but I didn't get a good look at him.

"Can you believe that?" I asked Oliver but he wasn't paying any attention to me, he was focused on the tailgate swerving down the road.

"What a jerk, he could've killed us." I said and that caught Oliver's attention.

"Are you okay?"

"Yeah, are you?" I asked. Oliver nodded.

"Wonder who that was?" He asked.

"Who cares?" I started pedaling toward home, my heart still pounding against my ribs. I didn't want to be there if whoever it was realized I'd flipped him off and decided to turn around.

"Are you coming?"

"I'm coming," he said but Oliver didn't come right away and I knew what he was doing, could tell by the sound of his voice. He was watching the taillights of the truck , worrying about the driver getting home safe.

"I hope he wrecks," I mumbled under my breath and didn't feel one bit guilty about it.

We snuck in the backdoor and into our bedroom without incident and put our pajamas on in the dark. I'd been so mad at almost being turned into roadkill, I'd forgotten to be anxious about our plan working until I got under the covers.

"What if the wind blows the note out of the flowers or that cat comes back and takes off with Mr. Trey's hat?" I asked. We still shared a room then, but it wouldn't last much longer. Mama had been trying to convince us that we both needed our own rooms for years, but I would cry and carry on until she stopped talking about it. I wasn't afraid of the dark unless I was by myself.

"Sissy, that ain't going to happen. Quit worrying."

"How do you know?"

"Because I just do. Goodnight." Oliver fell

Oliver

asleep as soon as his head hit the pillow.

Chapter Seven

Tonto never complained.

I finished my chores and helped Oliver sucker the last row of tobacco so we could get to the diner before Mr. Trey the next day. Ms. Linda had found the roses and had them displayed on the counter by the cash register. I was so proud of how they looked, I almost blurted out that we'd done it. To be safe I acted like I didn't see them. But it was hard because she was extra smiley and kept stopping to smell them and fuss over the Queen Anne's Lace. I could tell she wasn't worried about them having bugs which made me like her even more.

"Wow, Ms. Linda, those sure are pretty flowers," Oliver said. "They're almost as pretty as you."

"Flowers?" I looked everywhere but at the counter before I let my eyes fall on them. "Oh, those flowers. Dang, somebody must like you."

She beamed at us, so distracted she didn't even notice that we were there on a Wednesday.

We were halfway through our second round of root beer floats when Mr. Trey finally showed up. We'd never had two floats at one sitting before, but we couldn't leave until he got there. My stomach felt like it was about to explode when he walked in carrying his hat in his hands. Ms. Linda and Mr. Trey stared at each other for a second, then at the exact same time told each other thank you.

Then they both started to laugh. You could see Mr. Trey's shoulders relax from where we were sitting. He must've been a nervous wreck because he'd bent the brim of his hat all the way around. Then they stopped laughing and just stood there staring at each other again. It seemed like ten minutes went by and neither one of them moved.

Oh, for the love of Pete, we had to go! I had a stomachache from so much ice cream and root beer and if we didn't leave soon we'd be late for my favorite TV show. I walked up to the counter and cleared my throat.

"Oh, I'm sorry Olivia," Ms. Linda leaned over the counter to take my money. Her face was as red as the reddest rose in the jar. I looked at Mr. Trey. He was looking a little pale. I couldn't understand why grown-ups didn't just say what they wanted to say. It was obvious they needed more help.

"Ms. Linda, have you seen the new movie that's playing?" I knew she hadn't because it'd just opened.

"Uh, no. No, I haven't, Olivia." She was having trouble counting my change because she kept sneaking little looks at the flowers and Mr. Trey.

"Don't you want to?" I prodded.

She smiled at me. I turned to Mr. Trey and said, "Ms. Linda likes going to the movies."

He looked at me like he was seeing me for the first time, standing there abusing his poor hat.

"Do you like going to the movies, Mr. Trey?" He sort of raised one shoulder and maybe nodded, but I couldn't tell if that meant he liked going to the movies or if he was having the most boring conniption fit in history.

I threw my hands in the air and started walking to the door leaving Ms. Linda holding our change. I thought Oliver was right behind me, but he was still standing at the counter. I opened the door and gave it a shake to jingle the bell to get my brother's attention. Oliver took the change and started walking towards me, defeat written all over his face. As he reached the door the look of defeat was replaced with a mischievous grin, and he yelled over his shoulder, "Ask her to go to the movies!"

Mr. Trey turned toward Oliver, "Wha...?" Oliver turned and as the door shut between them, he yelled, "Ask her on a date! She likes to go to the movies!"

I grabbed his hand and we ran down the steps to our bikes. As much as I wanted to see what happened next, I had to get home. I pedaled as fast as I could despite the ice cream and root beer churning in my stomach. If two floats bothered Oliver you couldn't tell. He was grinning like a possum.

I dropped my bike in the driveway and ran inside to turn on the TV while Oliver parked his bike and mine beside the house. I was just about to lose patience with the rabbit ears and settle on the static when my brother came in. He adjusted the wads of tin foil wrapped around the pointy parts of the antennae and the static disappeared.

"How's that?" he asked.

I answered by shooing him out of the way, not even caring that it was rude because my stomach was killing me, and Tonto had just showed up on the screen. Oliver stretched out on his belly on the floor beside me, our noses about three feet from the screen.

The Lone Ranger was my favorite show. I didn't care that it was old, or that we were watching a rerun, or that all my friends thought it was boring, I loved it. Even though I knew how each episode was going to go, I still rooted for Tonto to be the hero, take some credit, or better yet, leave the Lone Ranger to fend for himself. Everybody knew that the Ranger would be lost without him. But Tonto never complained, and he would never let anybody mess with his friend no matter how full of himself he was.

Kinda like me and Oliver.

Chapter Eight

"No matter who we are, what we look like, or where we're from—that light shines on all of us."

Well, our plan worked! We saw Mr. Trey and Ms. Linda at the movies that weekend. Instead of her usual shade of pink, she'd painted her lips bright red for the occasion. I think Mr. Trey liked it because he couldn't take his eyes off her. Not even when Ms. Linda saw us and waved. I bet Mr. Trey didn't even know what the movie was about because all he saw was Ms. Linda. I know because I watched them instead of the movie.

"We should do something else like that," Oliver said later that night.

"Everybody else seems to do fine." I thought hard but couldn't think of anybody else who was in love but didn't know it.

"Not just like that, but something." Oliver looked around and I knew he was giving it some serious thought. "It felt good, didn't it? Seeing them holding hands? Ms. Linda has been going to the movies all by herself ever since I can remember. All Mr. Trey needed was a little help from us to get him going."

"Yep, but…"

"What if people just need a little push to notice each other?" He sighed. "To be a little nicer to each other?"

We were out riding our bikes a few days later when Oliver stopped in the middle of the road.

"Look, Olivia." He nodded towards Mr. and Mrs. Jones's front yard.

"What?"

"Mr. Jones used to do all the raking, but he got sick last year," Oliver said.

I remembered Mama saying he'd been in the hospital and the church had him on the prayer list for a whole month straight, but he'd come back and seemed okay. Except he had more white in his hair and used a cane.

Oliver

"Now look over there," Oliver nodded towards the next yard. "Mr. and Mrs. Shoulders's yard is all raked, but the hedges are scraggly."

I shrugged. I didn't know why Oliver was interested in their yards and I wasn't interested in finding out. I wanted to get to the drugstore and see if the new Archie comic had come in.

"I think we can help…"

I'm not going to lie. The first thought I had was to pedal away and hope Oliver forgot whatever he was thinking because the last thing I wanted to do was rake leaves. I hated raking leaves even for an allowance. But the look on Oliver's face told me that even if I took off he wouldn't stop thinking about whatever he was thinking.

"Alright already, what's the plan?"

Oliver smiled. "Come on, I'll tell you on the way to the drugstore."

I wasn't very happy to hear what Oliver had to say. His plan did include doing yard work that I hadn't been asked to do and would be doing for free. But Oliver got so worked up telling me all about it I didn't interrupt. Then he reminded me how much I liked sneaking out of the house at night and that was enough for me to agree.

We rode in front of the houses on the way home from the drugstore.

"See?" Oliver slowed down to stare at something behind the Jones's house. I had my comic book propped up in the basket attached to the handlebars and reading while I was coasting behind him, so I almost crashed into him.

"Dang it, Oliver, you need to pay more attention," I scolded. "See what?" I asked, irritated because I'd lost my spot.

"I think I see some hedge trimmers hanging up in there." The door to the small shed was open. "We won't even have to bring anything – see, there's Mr. Shoulders's rake," he pointed to the side porch on the other house. "It's like we're supposed to do it."

I gave him a half-hearted nod while I looked at the amount of leaves compared to the amount of bushes. There were just a couple of bushes but there were probably ten hundred thousand leaves.

"Well, I have to read this comic book before the next issue comes out so let's get moving."

"Okay, Grumpy," Oliver pushed against my calf with the front tire of his bike. He barely touched me, but I acted like it hurt and grinned when he looked shocked. He was such a sucker.

I took advantage of his big heart and pedaled off as fast as I could.

"Last one home has to rake the leaves!"

That night we waited until we heard the racket that was Daddy's snores and tiptoed out the back door.

I was still cranky but sneaking into Mr. Jones's shed lifted my spirits. It felt bad but not too bad...I mean the door was open, so I didn't feel too sneaky since the trimmers were hanging right there on the inside of the door, but I did feel a little bit sneaky, and I liked it.

We worked fast and I cussed under my breath using words we'd heard our Uncle Gene use but were told never to repeat. Maybe it was breaking into the shed that brought out the outlaw in me. Whatever it was I liked it probably more than I should and I was cussing up a storm by the time I finished the last bush. My arms were so shaky I could hardly hold the trimmers, but Oliver hadn't even broken a sweat and had the nerve to grin at me as he raked the last of the leaves into a pile.

When we finished, Oliver put the rake on Mr. Jones's front porch, and I put the trimmers on Mr. Shoulders's front porch. We hopped on our bikes and started home.

"Don't you feel good, Olivia?"

"I feel tired," I answered. "My damn arms are still shaking."

Oliver chuckled. "You better get all cussed out before we get home."

I scowled, but he was right. I knew we'd done a good thing, but what did it matter if nobody knew it was us? Getting Ms. Linda and Mr. Trey to go on a date had been fun. What we'd done tonight had been work. I didn't see the point.

"Just think about how surprised they're going to be in the morning." Oliver explained. "And Mr. Shoulders is young – maybe he'll keep raking their yard. Maybe he just never thought of it before."

"Or maybe he liked his bushes like they were, and Mrs. Jones liked the leaves in her yard."

Oliver laughed so hard he almost blew a snot bubble out of his nose, but I refused to laugh back. I was serious. Who was the first person who said you had to rake leaves anyway?

Oliver stopped right in front of me, and I slammed into him before I could hit my brakes.

"What is it?" All of a sudden I was thinking

about vampires and vampire bats and immediately felt bad for being grouchy with Oliver.

"Look at the moon, Olivia."

I looked up just in time to see it slide from beneath a cloud. I forgot to be ornery. You couldn't look at a moon like that and not feel good. Especially when you were with Oliver, who loved the moon so much Daddy called him Moonie.

Lots of people called Oliver Moonie instead of his real name. Daddy named him that when he was a little baby because Oliver stayed awake all night if there was a full moon. Mama and Daddy swear that Oliver would lie in his crib and coo at the moon and if he had a fit of colic or was cutting a tooth that was causing him pain, a full moon would calm Oliver right down.

Oliver talked about the moon like it was something made of magic. *Just think, Olivia – that same light that's touching you is touching everybody* – he'd say. *No matter who we are, what we look like, or where we're from —that light shines on all of us.* And don't even get him started talking about waxing and waning unless you want to hear about orbits, satellites, and how the moon effects the waves in the ocean. Oh, did you know that moonlight is actually sunlight that shines on the moon and bounces off? Me neither.

But I quit calling him Moonie when Eli Jones and those other jerks said he was named Moonie because his face looked like a moon pie. Moon Pie Face Moonie they called my brother. They said Oliver's face was round and flat, but it wasn't - they were just stupid. Stupid and useless.

I'd told Eli he was useless once. He'd made me mad and nothing I said would shut him up, he just kept laughing at my insults. But then I thought of something I'd heard Uncle Gene say about his old boss that caused Daddy to put his hands over my ears and send me off to play badminton. I always hung out with my uncles and peeled potatoes when we had fish fries, so I knew what Uncle Gene had said was too good to forget. Even though I had no idea what it meant, I'd filed it away. I figured it was a good time to use it.

I took in as much air as my lungs could hold and yelled as loud as I could, "Eli Jones – you're as useless as a knitted rubber!"

It did shut Eli Jones up, but it also got me a whipping when I got home because old Mrs. Diller came out of the drugstore right then and I yelled the insult intended for Eli Jones straight in her face. She dropped her purse to cover her mouth and stood there staring at me like I was the devil himself. I knew I was going to get in trouble, but the look on her face told me it was worth it. I bet she called to tell on me before her ears stopped ringing, because Mama met me on the sidewalk and whipped me with her wooden spoon all the way up the steps and into the house, yelling the whole time that she was going to make me take a bite out of a bar of Ivory soap. After she calmed down she forgot about the soap, but she didn't apologize about the whipping. You might think being whipped with a wooden spoon isn't bad but believe me, it stings. And it's humiliating because it's the same spoon she uses to scoop out mashed potatoes and creamed spinach at supper.

"Olivia Ann, if I ever..." but she was too wound up to finish and sent me to my room. She spent the rest of the afternoon taking a nap on the sofa while I sulked in my room.

Just thinking about that makes me mad all over again. Moon Pie Face...

Oliver isn't like me. He's never gotten one pop with the spoon or had to even lick the Ivory soap because he's always good. He never gets mad or cusses, and he even takes up for Eli because he and Eli used to be best friends – back when they were little. Before the other kids started making fun of Oliver and Eli got too embarrassed to be his friend. Oliver says that he feels sorry for Eli because Eli's daddy is mean when he drinks, and he drinks all the time.

I'd drink too if Eli Jones was my son, but I keep that to myself. I try to keep all the mean things I think to myself but sometimes I can't help it.

Like sometimes at Sunday School I say things that get me in trouble. Oliver always wants to talk to me about what happened even when Mama tells me she better not hear a word. Sometimes talking to him about it makes me feel better, but sometimes it doesn't. Like when I tried to ask why Noah was smiling on our coloring sheets. Ms. Thomas about had a hissy fit. I didn't say nothing bad, I just asked why he was so happy when everyone else was drowning to death?

Her answer was, "Olivia Ann. Put your head down and be quiet until I tell you to sit up." What kind of an answer was that? When I told Oliver what happened, he tried to explain that Noah's Ark was a story of hope. He loved the part about the dove and the olive branch, and he loved the whole thing about the rainbow.

Mrs. Clark had given him a book of stories about the bible for his birthday one year. It was as big as an encyclopedia and looked brand new, and boy did he love it. But it hurt my feelings and I refused to read it because for my birthday all she'd given me was a dogeared copy of *Are You There God? It's Me, Margaret* which was way smaller and somebody named Pamela had underlined parts and made notes in the margins.

"But everybody else died. Babies and old people. Dogs and cats."

"Sissy, you're looking at it the wrong way. Look at the good stuff," he insisted.

"But what do you think about all those people? Noah couldn't be the only person in the whole world who was good."

"It's just a story, Sissy," he said. "There's more to it than that."

"Well why don't they tell us the whole thing?"

He thought for a minute. "Because people get bored, and nobody would listen."

And the time I asked Ms. Thomas wasn't it wrong to blame Eve for Adam eating the apple when he was a full-grown man and he bit into it using his own free will. I was serious, we'd just learned about free will and why it was important but Ms. Thomas said she was tired of my silly jokes and made me sit out in the hallway – which was double punishment because it was the one that smelled like Elmer's glue and wet diapers – until Sunday School was over.

On the way home Oliver asked me what the matter was. By then I was mad and splotchy, which happens when I'm really mad, so he knew I'd been in trouble for something. He told me he thought the story about Adam and Eve was about making choices. I thought it was about two naked people who were sick of eating figs or whatever and a snake that was a troublemaker and nobody mentions the fact that Eve got punished for something she didn't even do, but I kept it to myself because I was too itchy to argue.

Chapter Nine

*Mama thought Ms. Robertson was
"inappropriate."*

A couple of days later Oliver and I were on our way home from the creek when we passed by a creepy looking house on the corner. I knew someone named Mr. Harrison lived there, because kids at school called it Mr. Harrison's Creepy House, but that's all I knew about it. It was the spookiest looking house in our neighborhood. Even the roses growing up both sides of the porch looked like something out of a scary movie because they were half dried up and nobody had ever removed the old roses. Most of them were black and hanging upside down.

"Hey, look," Oliver pointed to an old blue truck parked in the driveway of the house. "That's the…"

I waited for him to finish but he didn't. I'd never seen the truck before in my life. "The what?"

Oliver waved his hand. "Nothing."

I was looking at the roses when I thought I heard something. I motioned for Oliver to be still and strained to hear what sounded like somebody having a tantrum.

It was coming from the backyard of the house. It was still light out, so I felt brave and hopped off my bike. I motioned for Oliver to do the same and we tiptoed over to the fence.

"Sissy. Quit being nosy," he whispered, but I acted like I didn't hear him. I crept up and looked through the cracks between the weathered boards. It was getting dark quick, and it was shady back there, so it was hard to see at first, but once my eyes adjusted to the shadows I saw a man sitting at a picnic table. He was crying and drinking from a bottle.

"Boring," I whispered, lying. It wasn't boring, it was sad, and I didn't want to see anymore. I pulled on Oliver's sleeve to get his attention, but he swatted me, and kept staring through the crack in the fence.

I pulled harder and when he looked at me and I saw he had tears in his eyes. I was surprised to feel tears starting to form in mine and was afraid we'd both start bawling. Oliver is not a quiet crier.

I pointed at our bikes and tugged on Oliver's sleeve again. This time he followed me.

"Why is he crying?" Oliver asked, wiping his eyes.

I shook my head and waited for my eyes to dry up before I said anything.

"I don't know, but I know how to find out. We'll ask Ms. Robertson." Ms. Robertson was a cashier at the grocery store. If you wanted to find out anything about anybody in town, all you had to do was ask her. Mama always shooed us past Ms. Robertson when we went shopping with her because Mama thought Ms. Robertson was "inappropriate."

I thought she was great.

"We need to do something for him," Oliver said, and I got chill bumps on my arms. What could we do for somebody like that? We were quiet the rest of the way home. I couldn't stop thinking of old Mr. Harrison getting drunk and crying all alone in his backyard.

"Y'all alright?" Mama asked.

"Yes, ma'am. Just tired." We must've looked kinda pitiful because she didn't fuss at us for being late to dinner.

I felt tired, like Mr. Harrison had sucked all my energy out. He must've had the same effect on Oliver because we dried the dishes without hardly talking and neither one of us had to be told to go to bed on time.

"Goodnight, Oliver," I said when I got into my bed. He was already under the covers, and I thought he might be asleep.

"Goodnight, Sissy," he said, then turned over to face the wall. "We've got to do something for him."

We had no idea what we were getting ourselves into.

Chapter Ten

Maybe Mama was right...

After breakfast the next morning, we asked Mama if she wanted us to run to the Piggly Wiggly for her. Mama didn't like going to town unless she was made up. Today was laundry day, which meant she kept a kerchief on her hair and only put on lipstick right before Daddy came home, but she was always needing something from the store. You could count on that as sure as the sun was going to rise. Mama hated to be caught without a cup of sugar or a stick of butter to loan a neighbor if they asked – and she hated to be the one to borrow anything.

"Isn't that nice of y'all to offer – I have a list right here." She went to the notepad hanging by the phone. "Let's see…sugar, butter, and eggs."

I mimicked her behind her back and Oliver giggled as Mama told us to put it on her account. Why she always thought she had to remind us to put it on her account I couldn't figure out. Sometimes I thought she just liked saying it, like she was practicing for the day Daddy got rich and she would charge champagne and caviar at the Country Club on Sundays after church instead of coming home to cook fried chicken. I stopped and crossed my fingers when that thought crossed my mind. I closed my eyes and said a silent wish that one day it would happen. Mama always told Daddy she didn't care that they didn't have a membership to the Country Club whenever he brought it up, but I knew she did. I'd heard her on the phone with her friends talking about how nice it must be to be one of those couples after she'd gone to somebody's baby shower there. And she loved to dress up more than anybody I knew. She sewed three new mini dresses before that baby shower because she couldn't decide on which fabric she liked best. I sent a prayer out for good measure, *Please God or Jesus or Mary* (I never knew who to ask for a favor because God was probably busy with important things, so I liked to cover my bases even though I was raised Baptist) *make Daddy rich so they can join the Country Club. Amen.*

There wasn't anybody else grocery shopping, so we were in luck and had Ms. Robertson to ourselves. We put our things down in front of her at the cash register and I came right out and asked her if she knew Mr. Harrison.

"Mr. Harrison? Of course, I know Mr. Harrison. He lives over off Gum Street and drives an old blue Chevy pickup. Comes in here 'bout once a week for cigarettes and chewin' tobacco." She fluffed her hair that was permed to make it look thicker, but she also dyed it jet black so you could see her scalp around each tight curl. I thought her beauty shop lady should talk her into being a blonde, but I kept it to myself.

Ms. Robertson took another breath, "Nasty habit, that chewin' tobacco. Rerns your teeth. I had an uncle that used to have the purtiest teeth. Now when he smiles it looks like he has a mouth full of Indian corn. I think that's what it's called – you know that corn that has them kernels all different colors of brown, purple, black, yellow, and brown…it's a shame!"

She made a face at Oliver, and he laughed.

"Look at your nice teeth. Don't you go messin' them up now. Girls don't like boys with nasty teeth."

Oliver blushed, "Yes, ma'am."

"Does he live alone?" I wasn't about to let this go.

"Who, my uncle? No. He has a whole slew of women who don't care much about his teeth or theirs." Ms. Robertson made a face then let loose a cackle that made me jump.

"Oh, you mean Mr. Harrison? Since his wife died he does. He lives all alone and he's mean as a polecat. Why, I guess the only place he ever goes is to work and here to the Wiggly Pig."

"His wife died?" Oliver and I both asked at the same time.

"Oh, you sweet things, his wife and his son, both. Terrible shame. They both been gone awhile. He lost his son about a year before his wife, almost to the day. His son died over in Vietnam. He was just kid. Nice boy too, and handsome! Oh, he was a cutie pie. If I'd been twenty years younger, well…" She winked at me and fluffed her hair some more.

I looked at Oliver to see if he had any idea how to get her back on track and focused on Mr. Harrison, but he was too embarrassed to look at either one of us.

"How did his wife die?" I asked before she could tell us what she would've done if she was twenty years younger.

"His wife died from cancer. That Mrs. Harrison, she was a fine lady. Yes, ma'am, she was. Nicest woman I ever met. Why I bet you knew her – she was a regular over to the Baptist Church. Ain't that where y'all go? The one with that sexy hunk of a preacher? I've been a few times but it's too hard to get up early on a Sunday, even if Preacher Mark looks like Burt Reynolds. Naw, I get all the church I need on Wednesday nights at the Church of Christ in Springdale – and it's closer to my house. It's a pity to lose two loved ones so close to each other." Ms. Robertson was shaking her head and clucking like a hen. "Now I had an uncle who lost both his wife and a girlfriend in the same week. My uncle didn't know it, but his wife had been fooling around with his girlfriend's husband before he married her. I reckon that man thought he'd rather have his wife than my uncle's after all and took her down to live in Mississippi somewhere. Well, my uncle's wife took off after them! Last I heard the three of them all lived together happy as clams. Ain't that something?

Could you imagine losing your wife and your girlfriend to the same fella…at the same time?"

I stood there, wide-eyed, at a loss for words and waited for my change. Maybe Mama was right about her, but we did find out why Mr. Harrison was sad. I looked at Oliver to see if he was as shocked as I was to hear about Ms. Robertson's uncle, but I don't think he'd even heard the last part. He had on his thinking face, and I figured he was thinking only about what we could do for Mr. Harrison.

Chapter Eleven

"It hurt because it was true."

Doing something for Mr. Harrison became an obsession with Oliver. He talked about him nonstop and we'd taken to riding our bikes past his house at least once every day. We never saw him coming or going – or sitting in his back yard when we peeked through the fence. His house looked empty even when his truck was parked in the driveway.

I got tired of talking about Mr. Harrison all the time. I did feel sorry for him, losing his wife and son and all, but I didn't see that it was any of our business. Oliver didn't agree.

"He needs us," he'd say.

"He doesn't need us, Oliver. We're just kids. We can't go back in time and get his wife and son. It's not like it was with Ms. Linda and Mr. Trey. That was fun. This ain't fun at all. There ain't nothing we can do."

"We'll find something." Then Oliver said something that hurt my feelings, "You're just scared you're might have to do some work."

It hurt because it was true.

And then one day on our way home from delivering tomatoes to the ladies across the railroad tracks, Oliver found what he was looking for.

"Look, Olivia!" Oliver hollered and cut right in front of me

"Dang, Oliver, you almost made me wreck," I fussed. "You got the whole street. I don't know why you're always riding in front of me."

"But look…" Oliver pointed to the house across the street from Mr. Harrison's and before I could pedal off and ignore him for the rest of the day until he apologized, something caught my eye. There was a sign in the yard that said, "Free Puppies."

"I bet if Mr. Harrison had a puppy, he

wouldn't be so lonely," Oliver said, sounding hopeful.

The thought of looking at puppies almost made me forget I was aggravated, but then I remembered. And I remembered how tired I was of talking about Mr. Harrison.

"That's a dumb idea," I grumbled.

"No it ain't. Our other ideas worked. The last time we rode by Mrs. Shoulders's house, we saw Mr. and Mrs. Jones drinking lemonade with her on her front porch. And we saw Mr. Trey and Ms. Linda eating dinner at a fancy restaurant the other night." Oliver gave me a playful push on the shoulder. I was just being a brat – he was right, our other ideas had worked out great. We saw Mr. Trey and Ms. Linda when Daddy took us all out to dinner. He said it was to celebrate how good the tobacco was doing, but I thought it was an excuse to show off how good Mama looked in her favorite mini-dress.

She was so happy I even let her pull my hair back with a ribbon instead of a plain rubber band and Oliver wore his new penny loafers. Mama couldn't quit telling Daddy how handsome he looked, and she was right, he did. They were a good-looking couple, probably better looking than anybody at that old Country Club. Well, anyway, there were Mr. Trey and Ms. Linda - holding hands and everything. Oliver kept staring at them and waving until Daddy finally made him switch chairs with me, so they were behind him. I stared at them plenty, but at least I didn't wave.

"We need something to trade for the puppy. That's how it works. We can't take a puppy without leaving something," I said, giving in like he knew I would.

Oliver agreed and we sat on our bikes thinking. "I know! We could pick some of Mr. Harrison's roses and trade them for a puppy."

I studied the pitiful looking bushes from the street and was surprised to see a few not too dead looking roses that would work.

So we pedaled home and while Oliver was getting another mason jar and Mama's shears for the roses, I went inside to write a note for Mr. Harrison. Thinking about puppies put me in a better mood and I ran in my room to get the long piece of gold satin ribbon I'd worn in my hair when we'd gone out to eat. I cut it into two pieces, punched a small hole in the note and slide one piece of ribbon through it.

"Look! Ain't this pretty?" I asked Oliver when I got outside. "We'll tie this ribbon around the jar and this one around the puppy's neck."

He took the ribbon with the note on it and smiled. "That's perfect, Sissy."

We raced back to Mr. Harrison's house and got to work. Once I clipped some roses the bush looked better, so I forgot that I wasn't going to do any "work" and trimmed the whole bush back. It looked a lot happier, so I trimmed the second rose bush too.

Oliver picked up the piles of dead limbs and carried them to the curb. He came back smiling.

"That looks good, Olivia. See? Doesn't it feel good to do something nice for no reason?"

I had to agree. It did feel pretty darn good.

We filled the jar with the roses, tied the ribbon around the jar and made our way across the street. I set it on the porch in case there were any spiders hiding inside the petals while Oliver rang the doorbell.

A lady in a green housecoat with pink sponge rollers in her hair opened the door.

"Y'all here for a puppy?" she asked, but before we could answer she turned to look at her TV. I heard the familiar music and knew she was watching the same soap opera Mama watched. Her stories, she called them.

"Just go 'round back to the doghouse and

take your pick. Don't worry about the mama – she's in here with me," I looked around the lady and found a brown dog sitting on the sofa watching Guiding Light.

"She likes her stories too?" I asked, intrigued. The lady looked at me like I had two heads,

"Them pups 'bout drove her crazy. Once they was weaned she refused to go back out there."

I started to tell her that her dog sounded a lot like my Aunt Heather, but the lady shut the door in my face before I had a chance.

"Hey!" I turned to Oliver scowling, "She didn't even see the roses."

He laughed, "She'll find them later and be surprised."

We walked around back and found the puppies running around in a small pen, chasing each other, and digging holes in the dirt. Mr. Harrison would be home soon so we didn't get to play with them as long as I wanted, but that was alright. They were a little bit bitey anyway.

"No wonder your mama is sitting on the couch,"

I told the bitiest one and meant it. We picked out the cutest – least bitey – puppy and rode him across the street in the basket of my bike. Once we got to Mr. Harrison's yard, I tied the note that said "I'm lonely too" around his neck with the ribbon while Oliver held him. Then I kissed him goodbye on the top of his head real quick before he could get me with his sharp puppy teeth, and Oliver pushed him between two warped slats in the fence.

He didn't even bark. He went running around lifting his leg on everything in Mr. Harrison's back yard marking his new place and I could tell he was happy. I turned to Oliver to tell him how smart we were when I saw Mr. Harrison's truck turning the corner. He was driving too fast so his tires squealed against the pavement and I felt a shiver run up my back. I felt like I'd seen that before but I didn't have time to think about it.

"Let's go," I hollered. We got to our bikes just in time. Oliver and I circled the block and slowed down as we passed his house. I couldn't wait to see what happened next. Mr. Harrison's house didn't look so scary with the dead roses trimmed back and I pictured myself weeding Mr. Harrison's overgrown flower bed so I could play with his new puppy. Once he wasn't so sad.

We listened for a sign that Mr. Harrison had

found his new friend but didn't hear anything, so we circled the block again. We circled a couple more times and were about to give up when we heard a commotion coming from the backyard. Oliver and I turned at the end of the street at the same time Mr. Harrison came barreling through his back gate, carrying the puppy by the scruff of its neck.

He went straight across the street and stomped up the front steps of the house. As he went to knock on the door, he noticed the jar of roses. He turned to look at his house and saw where we'd trimmed the bushes, but instead of looking pleasantly surprised, he looked furious. I could barely breathe as I watched Mr. Harrison turn a deep shade of purple and I just about fell off my bike when he pounded on the door hard enough to knock the house numbers loose from the door frame.

I turned to Oliver, but he wouldn't take his eyes off Mr. Harrison. I looked back in time to see the lady in the green housecoat swing the door open. Mr. Harrison shook the puppy in her face before he threw him in the lady's arms, then he picked up the jar of roses and threw it in the middle of the street where it shattered in a million pieces. He started to say something to the lady, but either he was too mad to speak, or he changed his mind so he just glared at her instead.

She stood there still as granite, even when the puppy started nipping at her arms. I quess she was too afraid to move. Shoot, I would've been too. Finally Mr. Harrison left her porch, stomping and cussing all the way back home. I wanted to tell the lady I was sorry he'd been such a bully, but when she saw us on our bikes she slammed her door so hard it rattled the glass in her front window.

"Let's get the heck out of here," I said and started towards home.

Oliver rode up to where the jar had shattered in the street. He stopped to pick up the glass and called me back.

"Sissy, we can't just leave this here." I was embarrassed that I'd just rode by, but Oliver hadn't said it to make me feel bad. He just needed my basket to put the glass in.

"Why was he so mad?" I asked, but Oliver was as baffled as me.

When he'd gotten up all the glass he could, he picked up the piece of ribbon.

"You want this?" He held it up.

It had come untied and hung limp, wet with the water that used to be in the jar.

I shook my head, "No. It's gotta be bad luck."

Oliver turned to look at Mr. Harrison's house all the while wrapping and unwrapping the ribbon around his finger.

Finally he turned back to his bike and said, "I think it's got good luck in it. Feel it, it feels like it might have magic in it."

"Let's get out of here," I said, slapping his hand away.

Oliver slid the ribbon into his pocket, and I grinned in spite of how bad I felt imaging the ribbon in there with all of the other treasures Oliver carried around. He had a lucky rabbit's foot, a wheat penny, and a bookmark he'd made back when he was still young enough to go to Sunday school. It was creased in the center and worn thin where he'd folded it to fit in his pocket and one of the corners was torn off, but Oliver treated it like it was worth a hundred dollars.

There wasn't magic in it neither.

I knew Oliver kept it because it reminded him of his old Sunday school teacher Mrs. Carter. All the boys had loved her, and half of the daddies were known to make fools out of themselves over her too.

Oliver had cried when she left, but Mama

and her friends weren't sad one bit when pretty
Mrs. Carter and her husband moved to Kentucky.

Chapter Twelve

God probably doesn't believe in him neither...

After church the following Sunday, we drove our bikes past Mr. Harrison's house again. His truck was in the driveway, and I could smell something cooking on the grill in his backyard. I was scared, but I had to look. Oliver waited a second and then followed me over to the fence. We peeked in between the boards and saw him standing in front of a charcoal grill.

"What is it?" I whispered, letting my imagination get the best of me.

"Chicken," Oliver whispered back.

"Are you sure?" I wasn't. I thought it might be one of the puppies from across the street.

Oliver must have read my mind because he pointed out two drumsticks.

"Thank god," I said which struck Oliver's funny bone and we started giggling. Mr. Harrison heard us.

"I see you over there," he pointed straight through the space in the fence at me with a fork.

"What do you want?"

I had to think fast because if we took off running we'd look guilty as all get out. And he might figure out we were the ones who gave him the puppy.

"Hello? Is there anybody home?" I hollered but in a nice voice, trying to sound as innocent as I could. Oliver squeezed my arm.

"What are you doing?" Oliver whispered way too loud.

Mr. Harrison walked over and swung open the gate.

"That's what I want to know. What are you doing at my fence?"

I took a shaky deep breath and counted to three. "Hi there. I'm Olivia and this is my big brother, Oliver." He just stared at us. "We're looking for a few odd jobs to do over the summer," I almost choked on the words as they came out of my mouth.

Mr. Harrison turned back towards the grill and motioned for us to come through. We followed slowly and I rattled on and on about cutting the grass, picking up limbs, everything I could think of—without mentioning anything about trimming roses—while he moved the blackened pieces of chicken from the grill to a plate. Mr. Harrison let me talk while he picked up a glass and took a big drink. He made a face like it tasted awful and I wondered why he would drink anything that made him make a face like that.

"You two hungry?"

"No," I answered real quick.

"No, thank you," Oliver said, giving me a jab with his elbow.

"Well that's probably a good thing, because I bet this won't be worth eating no ways," Mr. Harrison said and he smiled, but it didn't look right. He looked sloppy, like his face was coming undone. "I ain't much of a cook."

I knew then that he was drunk because my uncles sometimes looked that way when we had fish fries. Right before my aunts said it was time to go–whether we'd eaten or not.

He sat down at the picnic table and mumbled about the sun being in his eyes. And it was—the table was sitting right in the one sunny spot of the yard.

Oliver asked, "Why don't you move it to the shade?"

He made a face like we were the dumbest people he'd ever seen, "How the hell do you think I could move the table all by myself?"

"I can help you." Oliver smiled and pointed to the perfect spot under a big oak tree.

Mr. Harrison stared at Oliver without saying anything. He took a bite, and I could tell it was tough. He took another bite and it looked like he was gnawing on a rubber chew toy. He finally gave up, threw the drumstick over the fence, and finished his drink. Then he got up and went inside.

"Let's go Oliver," I was almost to the gate when Mr. Harrison came back with a glass full of ice. He reached under the picnic table and picked up the same kind of bottle he was drinking out of the first time we'd seen him. He filled his glass and held the bottle out to Oliver. Oliver looked at him, his eyes wide and confused.

"No, thank you," he said.

"I guess not. What was I thinking?" He

slurred a little when he spoke and laughed like he'd said something funny.

"You know, if you want some good chicken, you should come to our church next Sunday. There's always chicken and those ladies sure do know how to cook it. They cook everything - pies, cakes, meatloaf, cookies…." Oliver nodded and smiled.

"Church? Hell no. Excuse me, no *thank you*." Mr. Harrison snickered then put his glass up to his mouth and drained it.

"They even make homemade ice cream and..." Oliver stopped talking as what Mr. Harrison had said sunk in. Where we lived, everybody went to church. Even Eli Jones.

"You don't go to church?"

"Nope, I don't. Used to, but then I found out it was a waste of my time." He stared at my brother without blinking.

"How come?"

"It's all a bunch of horse shit."

They stared at each other.

"It's not all…horseshit," Oliver said quietly.

"Yes, it is. Every bit of it. People think if they go to church and pray to some god all their cares will be washed away. Ha! What a joke. What God?" He poured another drink. "The God who took my son? The God who took my wife, even though she still believed in him, prayed to him when they told us that our boy was dead?"

He was getting really angry and the look in his eyes scared me.

"She never questioned him—your God. Never doubted him. And then you know what that God did? He gave her goddamn cancer. A nice big dose of it. Let her die a painful, horrible death. She kept on believing, kept on praying. Kept giving thanks to this wonderful life He had given her."

He was shouting now, "Never once did she stop believing. Never once did she question why. She kept on loving him even as she lay there in so much pain that she couldn't even open her goddamn eyelids."

He turned to look at my brother like he was seeing him for the first time. "Yeah, he's your God, too. What did he do for you?"

"He's done a lot...," Oliver started to answer but Mr. Harrison cut him off.

"You're a *re*tard boy," he sneered at my brother. "I bet you ain't got as much sense as a five-year-old—six on a good day. What are you going to do when your sister here moves on? She won't be around forever. Your Mama and Daddy will die one day, your sister will be married to some no good asshole and not have time for you, and what's your God gonna do for you then? Who's gonna give two shits about you when everyone you love is gone? God?"

Oliver didn't even flinch, but I couldn't take it. I let every cuss word I'd ever heard fly out of my mouth.

"Hell, he's smarter than you, ain't he – you stupid piece of shit! You ain't even got sense enough to move into the damn shade!" I yelled, my fear replaced with anger. "Shit, you'd rather sit in the damn sun and cry, you big, stupid, ugly…"

I didn't get to finish. With one hand over my mouth and the other arm around my middle pinning my arms against my sides, Oliver picked me up and headed for the gate. He knew how this worked; he had lots of practice.

Once I started, it took a while for me to stop.

He left our bikes where they were and carried me all the way home. After he got me inside and Mama had a cold washcloth on my face, he and Daddy went back for our bikes while Mama covered my arms and neck with calamine lotion. She didn't even ask me what happened, probably afraid of what I might say.

Halfway home my splotches had turned into full blown hives.

It was the first time I'd ever heard Oliver tell a lie. He told Mama that he'd been careless and run me into a ditch and embarrassed me in front of Eli Jones. It was pretty quick thinking on his part and made sense since I hated Eli Jones with every cell in my body.

That night as we were lying in our beds, I heard Oliver get something off the windowsill. At first I thought it was his worry rock, but then I caught a glimpse of gold and realized it was the piece of ribbon he'd stuck in his pocket..

"I can't stop thinking about Mr. Harrison," Oliver said as he pulled the ribbon tight between his thumb and forefinger, the satin strip taking the place of the smooth rock he usually fiddled with when something bothered him.

"Me neither. I can't stop thinking about choking his stupid neck," I said and meant it.

"You shouldn't be so mean, Olivia," Oliver said. "I can't stop thinking about him sitting there all alone—not believing in God."

"That's okay, because God probably doesn't believe in him neither," I said.

Oliver turned towards the wall and went to

Oliver

sleep without telling me goodnight.

Chapter Thirteen

He always goes through a hard spell this time of year...

After the incident with the puppy, we didn't look for things to do that meant getting in other people's business. We spent a lot of our free time down at the swimming hole, playing in the cold water, catching crawdads, looking for red-bellied salamanders, arrow heads, and all kinds of prizes. The old men who came to catfish on down on the other side of the bank loved to see us coming with our red plastic bucket full of crawdads. They swore it was the best bait for the fat channel catfish they liked to get - I didn't know if it was true or not, but the crawdads sure smelled a whole lot better than the chicken livers they used. They'd give us a dollar a bucket or offer us a chew of Red Man for a handful. I'd always act like I was going to take a chew and those old men would laugh and laugh. When Mr. Evans laughed, it made you feel good all over. He had the darkest skin and the deepest dimples I'd ever seen. There were a bunch of wrinkles around his eyes and mouth from laughing so much, and when he smiled his whole face lit up. I always wanted to stick my pointer finger in one of his dimples to see how far it'd reach, but I never did.

I'd almost forgotten about Mr. Harrison until we ran into him one afternoon at the Piggly Wiggly. Mama had asked us to run down to the store and pick up some sugar and there he was, standing right in front of us in the checkout line. I was trying to act like I'd forgotten something, but Oliver wouldn't let me get past him, so I fumbled with the magazines and acted like I didn't see Mr. Harrison even though he was right there.

If the truth be told, I was ashamed for the way I'd talked to him. He shouldn't have said those things about my bother—he's lucky I'm only a girl—but still, he was an adult. I'd never, ever talked to an adult like I had Mr. Harrison.

Oliver reached around me and tapped him on the shoulder.

"Cain't go wrong with bologna, can you, Mr. Harrison? You can fry it or eat it cold." Oliver smiled but when Mr. Harrison turned around, he acted like he'd never seen my brother before in his life. It didn't seem to bother Oliver at all; he kept right on talking, "Why, I bet you could even grill it. It wouldn't get too tough unless you flat out burned it."

Mr. Harrison grabbed the pack of bologna and loaf of Bunny Bread without waiting for it to be put in a bag and left without getting his change back from the cashier. Mrs. Martin put his thirteen cents on top of her register.

"Don't mind him none, Oliver. He always goes through a hard spell this time of year." She shook her head and patted Oliver's hand.

Ms. Martin wasn't a talker like Ms. Robertson, but she'd said plenty.

Chapter Fourteen

"I don't want to mess with him neither, Olivia. I want to help him."

A couple of nights later we were trying to go to sleep, but neither one of us were having much luck.

"Olivia?"

"Yeah?"

"I want to go back to Mr. Harrison's. He needs us.

"He needs to lay off the booze, that's what he needs," I said. We'd seen an old movie on PBS, my favorite TV channel of all times, with Humphrey Bogart in it and I'd been waiting to use that line. I pretended I had a cigarette between my fingers and took a puff.

"Well, we need to do something."

I propped myself up on my elbow so Oliver could tell I was serious. The light from the full moon coming through the window was so bright I could see him clearly in his twin bed across the room. "I don't want to mess with Mr. Harrison, okay? He's not right. There's something really wrong with him. Okay?"

"I don't want to mess with him neither, Olivia. I want to help him."

"Let's sleep on it and if we don't come up with something overnight, we'll just forget about him, okay?" I crossed my fingers under the covers.

"Okay," Oliver sighed. "Good night, Sissy."

"Good night. Now go to sleep." I wanted him to stop thinking so hard about what he could do for Mr. Harrison, but he was fiddling with that piece of ribbon and his eyes were wide open. I knew he'd be up a while longer.

I rolled over to face the wall and pulled my pillow over my head to make it as dark as possible. I wanted to go to sleep so I'd stop thinking about the way Mr. Harrison looked at us, like he didn't see us. I'd never seen eyes like that before. Before I'd met Mr. Harrison, I'd never met anybody who had nothing to live for.

The whole next day passed without any word about Mr. Harrison and I was so relieved that when it was time for bed I fell asleep as soon as my head hit my pillow. But I hadn't been asleep long when I felt Oliver shaking my arm.

I thought I was dreaming because the moon was so bright it seemed to be in our room and Oliver looked like he was glowing. He looked like a real life super hero.

"Moonie...?" I whispered and realized I was awake.

"Come on Olivia." He shook me again.

"Where are we going?" I asked, but I already knew the answer.

I got dressed without protest but stepped on all the creaky spots in the hallway hoping Daddy or Mama would wake up before we made it outside. If Oliver noticed what I was doing he didn't say anything. It didn't matter anyway because Daddy's snores were so loud I could've gone up and down the hall on my pogo stick reciting the National Anthem and nobody would've noticed. Oliver waited for me to get on my bike and follow him. He stopped on the curb in front of Mr. Harrison's house and held up his hand to shush me before I said anything.

"Don't say it. Don't say that you don't want to come here, because he needs us, I know it. I feel it." He was whispering loudly and making all sorts of gestures with his hands like he couldn't control them and they had a mind of their own. Like he used to do when he was little and got overly excited. "I mean it, Olivia."

"Let's peek and see if he's out there, but that's all, okay?" I sighed.

He leaned his bike against the kickstand and hugged me, then we crept up to the fence.

We heard him before we saw him.

Mr. Harrison was sobbing and talking to himself. I couldn't make out everything he was saying, but whatever it was, it was pitiful. We found the widest crack in the fence and pressed up against it, trying to get our eyes to focus. Right then the moon came out from behind a cloud and the light shone down through a bare spot in the biggest oak like a spotlight directed right at Mr. Harrison. My heart stopped beating.

There was a shotgun on the table. Beside the gun was a box of shells and a whiskey bottle. Mr. Harrison raised his glass up at the sky.

"I tried to keep my promises, but I'm not strong like you." He threw his glass right towards us where it hit the fence and exploded into a hundred pieces. We froze, so still we could barely breath. "Just give me a sign. One sign. I need something, Lenore, or I'm…"

He picked up the shotgun and put the stock on the ground. Then he sat up straight and put the barrel under his chin. I thought I might throw up when he leaned forward and pressed the barrel of the shotgun deep into his skin.

"Do you think he's going to…?" Oliver whispered.

"Yes, I do." I took his hand and turned to run to our bikes. "We need to get Daddy."

Oliver startled me when he yanked his hand away. "No. We need to do something *now.*"

Before I could ask what he thought we could do, Oliver ran around the house and up the front steps. He rang the doorbell and banged on the door at the same time. I put my fingers in my ears expecting to hear the loud bang of the gun, but I saw Mr. Harrison's shadow moving to the back door. When I heard it open I hollered to Oliver.

"He's coming!"

Oliver ran past me and through the back gate. Before I had time to think about what we were doing I was at the picnic table beside my brother. Oliver picked up the shotgun and accidentally knocked the bottle of whiskey to the ground.

"Oh, shit!" I hissed and turned to run. He grabbed hold of the back pocket of my shorts to stop me.

"Here." He handed me the gun and I pointed it towards the ground. I didn't like holding it but what could I do?

Everything seemed to be happening in slow motion.

"Oliver, we got to get out of here." I was expecting Mr. Harrison to come out the door any second.

"We need to leave something. We never took anything without leaving something before. It don't feel right."

I was about to pee my pants. It felt like time had come to a dead stop. I didn't know how long we'd been standing there, but I knew it was too long.

"I got it!" Oliver reached in his pocket, pulled his good luck charms out, and put them where the shotgun had been just seconds before. A breeze came out of nowhere and sent Oliver's tiger-eye marble rolling off the table where it bounced across the patio. The marble caught the light of the moon and it shot little streaks of orange and red light against the dull concrete before the moon slid behind another cloud. I wished Oliver had seen it, but he was too busy putting everything else under the whiskey bottle to keep from blowing away. Right then the moon shone down again, this time on Oliver. It hit the piece of gold ribbon, and sent a spark of light across the table and brought me back to my senses.

"Oliver, please, come on…"

He took the shotgun out of my hands, and we ran as fast as we could. I kept up with Oliver, which surprised me considering my legs were shaking so bad my knees were almost knocking. We heard the back door open just as the gate closed. I expected to feel Mr. Harrison's hand grab me up by my neck and carry me back into his yard like he'd carried the puppy across the street, but he didn't come through the gate. I didn't slow down until I reached my bike.

Before I could take off, Oliver switched the safety on and slid the barrel of the shotgun through a hole in the side of the basket on my bike. I'd never even noticed the hole before, but it fit the barrel of the gun like it was made for it.

Chapter Fifteen

*Somehow Oliver always knew
exactly what to do.*

We pedaled our bikes for all we were worth.

Oliver kept on going instead of turning in the driveway of our house and I had to pedal hard to catch up with him. I didn't know where we were going, and I didn't care. I just wanted to get as far away from Mr. Harrison as I could.

When we reached the bridge that crossed Carr Creek, Oliver let his bike fall to the ground and pulled the shotgun out of my basket before I'd come to a full stop.

"What are you..." I started to ask but Oliver answered me by throwing the gun into the water.

I hopped off my bike and ran to look over the concrete railing, but by then I was crying so hard I couldn't see anything. I don't know if I was crying because I was scared or because I was sad, or both. Oliver hugged me tight and patted my back until I was able to stop.

"Come on, Sissy, let's go home."

Once we'd gotten back home, safe and sound in our beds Oliver said, "That's a good thing we done, Olivia."

But I wasn't so sure. I thought what we did made everything worse. Now Mr. Harrison had a reason to be mad at us. What would he do when he figured out we took his gun? We'd left proof that we were there! Would we go to jail? I didn't think I would ever go to sleep. I kept going back and forth between worrying about getting in trouble and wondering what would've happened if Oliver hadn't been so set on going over there. Would Mr. Harrison really have done it? Who would've found him? How long would he have been out there all by himself?

The next morning was Sunday. I hadn't been able to stop thinking about everything and had tossed and turned for hours. Once I fell asleep I was out like light. I overslept so everybody was already in the kitchen when I got up. Oliver looked like he'd slept fine, but I couldn't ask him anything without making Mama curious. I thought about playing hooky from church—but I didn't want to be left at home by myself. So I ate breakfast real quick and got dressed.

We'd barely gotten seated in the hard oak pew when Mama began making a fuss over me, feeling my forehead and patting my knee. I usually liked all the attention, but I felt like a big phony that morning. What did I have to feel bad about? I had my family. Mr. Harrison didn't have anybody. I looked over at Oliver and thought how I would feel if he was taken away from me. If he got shot in Vietnam or got sick and died because of cancer. I'd hate everybody too.

"Look, Olivia," Oliver whispered loud enough for everybody on our side of the church to hear. We all turned to see what he was talking about, and I swear everyone froze. You could've heard a pin drop.

"Well, I'll be," Daddy mumbled to Mama who sat there with her mouth open.

Even the preacher couldn't hide the surprised look on his face as he watched Mr. Harrison take a seat in the last row. I heard people whispering all around us.

"It's about time he made good on his promise..."

"...this would make Lenore so happy."

"Look - what's he holding?"

"It's the ribbon Lenne used for a bookmark... "

"No..."

"Yes, ma'am. She made a slew of them for our bible study group..."

"It sure looks like it..."

"See, I still have mine..."

I turned just in time to see Mrs. Freeman slide a piece of gold satin ribbon from the pages of her bible. *"She used up all the left over ribbon from the hristmas pageant.."*

"Remember, her son was a wise man..."

"Poor little Robbie..."

"She carried a strip with her everywhere she went..."

I felt a chill shoot up from the soles of my feet and shivered when it went up my spine.

Oliver squeezed my hand, "I told you it was magic. I could feel it."

"Let us pray," Preacher Mark said, and everyone turned to face the front.

I bowed my head and closed my eyes, but I couldn't hear what the preacher was saying. I was too busy thinking about the night before, the way the light hit the piece of ribbon when Oliver put it on the table.

I opened my eyes to look at Oliver. His head was bowed, his eyes were closed, and he was smiling so big I had to smile myself. I snuck a look at Mr. Harrison over my shoulder, brave enough to look because I thought his eyes would be closed in prayer, but he wasn't praying. He was staring straight at me.

Our eyes locked on each other and I couldn't turn away. He didn't look happy, but at least he looked like he felt something other than hate. He nodded, which seemed to break whatever spell I was under. I didn't know what it meant, but I nodded back and hoped he knew mine was an apology for being so disrespectful. And not paying attention. And for being so selfish. And especially for stealing his shotgun.

I turned around, closed my eyes, and said my own silent prayer.

"Dear God…and Jesus and Mary, thank you for my daddy and my mama, even when she's flaring her nostrils, and for my brother, and for magic. I'm sorry I don't always see it, but I promise I'll try harder. And I'm sorry I'm so angry and lazy and mean sometimes. And I'm

sorry I like to cuss – I'll try harder on that too. Amen."

"Amen. Let's open the hymnbooks to page eighty-six," Preacher Mark instructed.

As everyone found their places, Oliver leaned over and gave me a nudge. "Here, Sissy, this is for you."

I held out my hand and Oliver dropped something in it. It was his lucky tiger-eye marble.

"How in the…?" The last time I'd seen it, it was bouncing out of sight somewhere in Mr. Harrison's yard.

Oliver winked, "Magic."

Acknowledgments

I love this part! The only bad thing is that I don't have room to thank everybody individually, so I'll start with the person who pushed me to make time for myself to write in the middle of a busy schedule. The fabulous Robert Gwaltney.

I was able to finish Oliver thanks to his encouragement and friendly nudges to get up at 4:30 in the morning. I looked forward to his "Morning!" texts and to our check-in chats at 6:30am to see how we did. You know, he's a brilliant author. He spent the mornings working on an epilogue and the final edits of his debut novel which made this even more special. If you haven't read *The Cicada Tree*, you need to put it on your to be read list right now.

A big THANK YOU to Carolyn Haines - an extremely talented author and all around beautiful human being. She saw a post on FB where I said I was writing a novella. She asked to read Oliver when it was in its first stages and y'all I can't even explain what that meant to me. When I sent it to her she asked if I'd like her to edit it. Heck yeah! How could I turn down an offer from a Harper Lee Award recipient? One who's been inducted into the Alabama Writer's Hall of Fame no less... I'm still pinching myself. How'd I get so lucky?

I want to thank my BFF, Pamela Lambiase. We used to spend Thursdays on her deck back in Nashville and she always read my stories before they were finished. It's different now - I live in Florida and she moved to Hurricane, Utah. No more deck nights drinking tequila and solving the worlds problems while my three dogs are spoiled rotten by the fire -but she's still my first reader! Thank you Pammie! We love you to the moon and back.

Thank you River Jordan for all of the encouragement! From sharing hilarious TikToks to DoorDash Liquor deliveries from 900 miles away you keep me laughing. I mean it from the bottom of my heart when I say *Wish You Were Were.*

Thank you Claire Fullerton for your read through and red ink marks. Lord, I hate commas ... You were so sweet to offer your help and it was much appreciated. You're right - it takes a village!

Most importantly - thank you readers!

A special shout out to Ruth Benson and Pam

Durkee-Carmichael. Two wonderful reader friends I've made on social media who check in on me and always make me feel special. They are always cheering authors on on Facebook and it tickles me every time I see their names pop up! Thanks to every fellow author who takes the time to read my stories -I know your free time to read is precious, so it's really something when I see a review or post from ya'll about my stories!

Last but not least, I want to thank Kathy L.Murphy for talking me up when I need it the most. Thank you Kathy for everything you do for us authors. YOU are the diamond in all of our tiaras.

Reader's Guide for Oliver

1. I knew a couple, Clyde and Elizabeth, who lived in my hometown. Clyde was the janitor at our school and Elizabeth worked in the cafeteria. They were married and walked to and from work every day on the side of the main highway (not much more than a two lane street back then) holding hands. Every day. They both had some kind of "developmental disability" (I hate even typing that) but they lived together as man and wife in their own house and enjoyed life. I loved watching for Clyde and Elizabeth on the way to school and always wanted to know more about them. Years later I was fortunate to meet lots of kids with different "disabilities" in the sixteen years I worked in pediatric cardiology. Many of them were extremely intelligent and high functioning kiddos who would grow up to be independent adults. The ones who did the best had siblings like Olivia who didn't treat Oliver different than anyone else - and parents who refused to label them. Oliver is a fictional character, but he is a mix of all of these people I was lucky to meet. Did know someone

like Oliver in your school or in your hometown? Someone a little different who was bullied and that people made up stories about?

2. What were you doing in 1972?

3. I love reading a story where a character reminds me of myself, a friend, or family member. Olivia reminds me so much of me as a kid - the good the bad and the ugly parts - that she was a blast to write. Did she remind you of yourself or someone you know?

4. How are Olivia and Oliver different from one another?

5. What traits do they have in common?

6. Olivia is set in her ways, but thanks to Oliver she gets friendly nudges to do better in lots of ways. Would she find compassion for others without him?

7. Did Olivia or Oliver remind you of your siblings in any way?

my Aunt Hazel lived so we always had fresh sun

8. Did you have a special bond with a sibling when you were young? If so, do you still have it?

9. Is there a time in your life where a stranger showed up and changed the way you were feeling? Maybe something as small as a smile when you were feeling sad or an impromptu conversation in the checkout line at a grocery store when you were feeling lonely?

10. Has there been a time when you where that person for someone else?

11. Did the story bring back memories of your own childhood? Did you go creeking? Catch crawdads and salamanders? Did you ride your bike everywhere?

12. When you were young, were there adults like the old men who loved to catfish, or the ladies Olivia and Oliver delivered vegetables to that you liked visiting?

13. Fish-fries were a big thing in my family growing up. My Uncle Woodard had a couple of ponds on the property where he and

perch and brim to fry in the summer. We had barbecues too, but there's something special about a fish-fry. Neighbors you've never met show up! Have you ever had a fish fry in your backyard?

14. Has there been a time in your life where you thought something tragic was about to happen in someone's life and you stepped in, not knowing what would happen? If so, how was your support received?

15. Has there been a time that you didn't, but wished you had?

16. When you were a kid, what was your most prized possession? Did you have a lucky rock or favorite marble that you carried around with you?

17. High School Football games are the place to be on Friday nights in so many small towns. Is that true where you live?

18. Mrs. Catherine Clark, the librarian in the story, is the real name of my elementary school librarian. She is a professional storyteller and

beautiful woman who loved the color purple, but on Halloween she transformed into the scariest witch you ever saw and gave us all nightmares from the stage of the auditorium. She was the highlight of my elementary school days and I couldn't wait for library days and story time with Mrs. Clark. Do you remember your elementary school librarian?

19. This is just for fun - If you read my first collection, Walking the Wrong Way Home, you met Penny in the story The Red Shoes. Did you happen to catch the reference?

Thank you so much for reading Oliver. I had the short story version tucked in a file for years just waiting for the right place. I even tried to turn it into a novel once, but it felt too forced so I stepped away. But months spent hunkering down waiting for this virus to peter out, we readers are reading more than ever - and readers are reading novellas again. So I dug Oliver and Olivia out from under stacks of stories and story ideas and finally gave them their spotlight. I'm so glad I did! I had too much fun writing in Olivia's voice. We're a lot alike - some of the things she mentions are actually things I did. Ask my mama about finding dried up bits of unidentifiable vegetables on the ledge under her farmhouse dining table. That was not a good day...

I'd love to meet you! Please drop me a line at www.mandyhaynes.com or find me on Facebook www.facebook.com/mandywrites

If you're in a book club or have a group of book loving friends who'd like to get together to talk about Oliver I'm just a Zoom link away.

ps If you leave a review on Amazon or Goodreads when you finish reading, I will do a happy dance in your honor! If you're on social media - I might just tag you in it so be ready to dance with me!

CPSIA information can be obtained
at www.ICGtesting.com
Printed in the USA
JSHW051932240222
23274JS00004B/15